Two-Minute Bedtime Stories

By MARY PACKARD
Illustrated by KATHY WILBURN

For Jane, who loves books and little animals

A GOLDEN BOOK • NEW YORK
Western Publishing Company, Inc., Racine, Wisconsin 53404

Little Redcoat Takes a Trip

Little Redcoat woke up in a wonderful mood. There was a nip in the air, and he could hear the autumn leaves rustling outside his window.

"It's a perfect day to play hide-and-seek," said the young cardinal to his mother. "I'll hide behind a cluster of red leaves and no one will ever find me!"

He quickly finished his breakfast and flew off to find his friends.

He heard Rusty, the robin, chirping on a branch.

"One, two, three, four," Rusty sang. He flapped his wings up and down to the beat of his song.

"Want to play hide-and-seek?" asked Little Redcoat.

"I can't," said Rusty breathlessly. "I'm in training to make my wings strong. Tomorrow my family is flying south for the winter."

"Oh," said Little Redcoat thoughtfully. "South...I've never been there."

"It's wonderful!" said Rusty. "The sun is warm and the trees are green all year long."

So Little Redcoat left Rusty to train and flew off to find Blaze, the sparrow.

Blaze was having breakfast in a huckleberry bush.

"Do you want to play hide-and-seek?" Little Redcoat asked.

"I don't have time," she answered. "I'll be eating all day. Tomorrow my family is flying south, you know."

That night at home Little Redcoat said, "How come we never go anywhere? Everybody takes trips but us."

"It takes more than a few snowflakes to scare us away," said his father. "We don't need to fly south for the winter. Cardinals are strong and hardy," he added proudly.

"And boring," muttered Little Redcoat under his breath. "What I need is some adventure," he said loudly. "I want to fly south with Rusty and the other birds tomorrow."

Little Redcoat's parents looked at each other. "You're old enough to do as you like," said his father quietly. "But remember, there's no place like home."

The next morning Little Redcoat got up early. He went to meet Rusty at the Redbreast Resting Place, a telephone wire that stretched clear across the meadow. Before he knew it, Little Redcoat was on his way south.

It seemed like the trip took forever. Little Redcoat's muscles ached. Even his feathers ached. "It will all be worth it when I finally get to see south," he said to himself.

At last the trip was over. "We're here!" the birds cheered.

"So this is south," said Little Redcoat in a disappointed voice. Except for a few palm trees, it didn't look very different from his own home in the summer.

Little Redcoat missed his family. He was so tired from the long flight that he took a long nap. He dreamed of pine trees, snow drifts, and cozy winter nights at home with his family.

When he awoke, Little Redcoat had made up his mind. "Time to head home," he said.

Little Redcoat arrived just in time for the first snowfall. And he was very glad to see his family again. "Home really is the best place of all!" he chirped happily.

Barnaby's Bad Dream

Barnaby Bear could not fall asleep. His mother had checked under his bed for monsters three times. She had read him four bedtime stories and brought him two glasses of water. But the little bear still couldn't fall asleep.

"Mummy!" he called. "There's a monster in my cupboard!"

"I doubt it," said Barnaby's mother. Then she opened the cupboard door to prove her point. Everything Barnaby owned was stuffed in there, and it all came tumbling out at her feet.

"On second thought, who could tell what's living in here?" she said. "A monster who likes messes would certainly be very comfortable here! Now, good night, Barnaby!"

"I'll never get to sleep now," thought Barnaby. "What if there really is a monster living in my closet? I guess I'll have to look myself."

Carefully stepping over the clutter, Barnaby cleared a spot so he could sit on the closet floor. He started to sort through his stuff. There were dirty clothes, toys, books, games, shoes, and old candy wrappers. There were things in there that he had nearly forgotten about—like his toy beehive and his rock collection. As he started to pick up his old baseball cap, Barnaby heard a voice.

"Hey, leave that alone!"

Barnaby carefully peeked underneath the edge of the cap. To his surprise a pair of tiny eyes attached to a little fuzzy body stared back at him.

"Who are you?" asked Barnaby.

"I'm a Messter," said the creature. "Messters love messes. And this was one great mess until you showed up! Who are you, anyway?" the Messter demanded.

"I'm Barnaby," he said. "And this is my cupboard."

"Not anymore," growled the Messter. "We're taking over!"

All of a sudden Barnaby's cupboard came alive with hundreds of twinkling eyes and scary voices.

But one voice was louder than all the rest. Barnaby felt someone shaking him.

"Barnaby! Barnaby!" said his mother. "Wake up you silly bear! You're having a bad dream."

"Whew!" Barnaby said. "Was it ever! I'm glad it was just a dream!"

"Why are you sleeping in your cupboard?" his mother asked.

"Oh, I just wanted to get a head start cleaning it," Barnaby said. "After all, you never know what might be hiding in there!"

Melody's Miserable Morning

Melody Mouse was having a miserable morning. She had washed her favorite doll's hair and all of the doll's beautiful curls had come out! Then Melody had drawn a picture of her baby brother.

"What a lovely cat, Melody," her mother said. Melody groaned.

"I guess I just can't do anything right today," she said sadly.

Melody decided to take a walk to cheer herself up. In the pasture, she saw her friend Carlotta the cow.

"How are you today?" Melody asked politely.

"Not so well," said Carlotta. "While I was rolling in the grass I must have picked up a thorn, and I can't reach it to pull it out."

"I'll help you," said Melody. She dashed up the fence post and hopped onto Carlotta's back. She quickly found the thorn and pulled it out.

"That feels so much better!" Carlotta said. "I'm so glad you came by."

"No trouble at all!" said Melody, and she continued on her walk.

It wasn't long before she saw her old friend Clancy, a colour-blind chameleon.

"How are you?" asked Melody.

"Same old problem," said Clancy. "It happens every fall. The leaves change colours so quickly, I have trouble blending in. Could you tell me what colour leaf I'm on?"

"No problem," said Melody. "It's a red maple leaf."

"Gee, thanks," Clancy said, slowly turning red all over.

"You're welcome!" said Melody.

Melody followed a trail through the woods and walked right into Woodruff Squirrel. He was scampering from one tree to another.

"What's wrong?" she asked.

"I hid my acorns and now I can't find them!" wailed Woodruff.

"Don't worry," said Melody. "I'm good at finding things." In no time at all, Melody had gathered a big pile of acorns.

"You're a good friend, Melody," said Woodruff gratefully. "I never would have found my acorns without you."

The sight of Woodruff chomping on his acorns reminded Melody that she hadn't eaten any lunch. She started walking back home and thought about all the helpful things she had done.

"This hasn't been such a terrible morning after all!" said Melody as she skipped happily home.

Owl's Birthday Party

One afternoon all the woodland animals who lived in Chestnut Hollow gathered beneath the tallest tree in the forest.

High above them they could hear Owl snoring loudly in his snug little house. It was Owl's birthday, and everyone was there to get ready for the party they had planned for him.

Chauncy Chipmunk and Samuel Squirrel were painting pinecones to string through the trees.

"Wait until Owl sees the book I got him," said Samuel. "It's called the *Who's Who Book of Famous Owls*. I just know he's going to love it."

"Ssh!" whispered Helga Hedgehog. "We don't want to wake Owl up and spoil his surprise. By the way," she said quietly, "do you want to see what I'm giving Owl?"

Helga held up two strange knitted sweaters. "What are they?" asked Chauncy.

"They're wing warmers, silly," said Helga. "Owl can use them when he flies on cold winter nights."

"That's a great gift," said Chauncy. But Chauncy was sad, for try as he might, he still had not thought of a present that was fine enough for his special friend.

As he decorated the pinecones Chauncy thought about all the wonderful things Owl had done for the woodland animals.

He remembered the time that Fritz Fox had grabbed Chauncy's lunch box on the way to school. Fritz devoured all the acorns Chauncy had packed for lunch. It was Owl who thought of filling some acorns with hot peppers the next day. When Fritz stole Chauncy's lunch again, the greedy fox was in for an unpleasant surprise. Fritz never bothered Chauncy again.

And it was Owl who had taught the woodpeckers how to tap out emergency messages in code. Three short taps followed by two long taps meant "Fire." Two long taps followed by three short ones meant "Flood."

"What can I get Owl to show him how much he means to me?" thought Chauncy.

Ramona Rabbit had just finished setting the table. It looked lovely, with party favours at every plate and a seven-layer birthday cake as a centrepiece.

"It's a good thing Owl sleeps all day," Ramona said, "or we never could have made everything ready."

"You don't have to worry about Owl getting up," said Polly Porcupine. "The sun hurts his eyes, you know."

"That's it!" exclaimed Chauncy. "I know just what to give Owl for his birthday!" Chauncy raced back to his house as fast as he could.

When he got home, Chauncy found his trunk of old Halloween costumes. He rummaged through the trunk. "Where are they?" he cried. "I know they're in here somewhere. I wore them last year when I dressed up as a movie star."

Finally Chauncy found what he was looking for. He wrapped the gift in bright paper, and then he hurried back to the party.

By then the sun had gone down. Owl was just waking up.

"Surprise!" the woodland animals shouted. "Happy birthday!"

"What's all this?" said Owl happily. "A surprise party for me?"

Owl opened the gifts one by one. "They're all so nice," he said. "Thank you all very, very much!"

"I saved mine for last," said Chauncy as he handed Owl the gift.

Owl opened the present. "Sunglasses!" he cried. "That's exactly what I need!"

"Now you can fly around in the daytime and the sun won't hurt your eyes," said Chauncy.

"Thank you, Chauncy," said Owl. "This is a very thoughtful gift. I'm lucky to have such good friends," he added.

And then they all sang "Happy Birthday" and sat down to eat some cake.

The Raccoon Kids Go to Town

One afternoon Rebecca, Rodney, and Rory Raccoon had to go to the market to buy groceries. Their mother couldn't do the shopping that day because she had a cold.

"Here's your bus fare," she said, "and here's the grocery list. Now, be sure to get home before dark."

"Don't worry, Mama," they said. "We'll be careful."

When they got to town, the raccoon kids went straight to the market and bought everything on the list. Since it was a while before the bus would take them home, they walked up and down the street, looking in shop windows.

"They still have that dressing table set that Mama wanted the last time we came to town," Rory said.

Rebecca stared at the brush, comb, and mirror. They were very beautiful, with wooden handles and hand-painted flowers.

"Look," said Rodney. "The set is on sale!"

Then Rory had an idea. "If we walk home instead of taking the bus," he said, "we could buy Mama the set as a special get-well present."

"Let's do it!" they all agreed.

Five minutes later they came out of the shop with Mama's present wrapped up in pretty pink paper and a polka-dot bow.

As they started walking home the three raccoons talked about how happy Mama would be when she saw her surprise. It seemed they had walked a very long way when they reached Old Man Ferret's farm.

"How much farther?" asked Rebecca. "These groceries are getting heavy."

"We're not even halfway home yet," moaned Rory, whose arms and feet were also aching.

FERRET

"It's getting awfully dark," said Rodney. Suddenly there was a bright flash of lightning and a loud clap of thunder. It started to pour.

"Oh, no!" cried Rebecca. "What will we do now?"

Just then a car pulled up beside them. Aunt Rosie was driving.

"Would you kids like a ride?" she called to them.

"Would we ever!" said the three raccoons. They quickly jumped in the car. "The walk from town was a lot longer than we thought," said Rodney.

"I hope our mother's not too worried," said Rory.

"Thank goodness you're finally home!" cried Mrs. Raccoon as her children walked in the door. "I've been so worried about you!"

"We're sorry we're late, Mama," said Rory. "It's just that we decided to walk home."

"All the way from town?" Mrs. Raccoon said.

"Here's why we didn't take the bus, Mama," said Rebecca as she handed her mother a soggy present.

"Oh, how beautiful," said Mrs. Raccoon when she saw what was in the box. "It's just what I wanted!"

She gave her three little raccoons a big hug. "I feel better already!" Mrs. Raccoon said. And that's just what Rebecca, Rodney, and Rory were hoping she would say.

The Legend of the Ring-tailed Rabbit

"Tell us another story, Grandma," begged Hazel and Hilary Hopkin, two frisky little rabbits who would do anything to stay up past their bedtime.

"Well, I guess one more wouldn't hurt," said Grandma.

"When I was a very young rabbit, before I met your grandpa," she began, "I went to the Cottontail Ball. I had on a brand-new gown, and I looked beautiful—if I do say so myself. Of course, every young hare had to have a dance with me that night. And I had a wonderful time as they whirled me round and round the dance floor.

"But all that dancing made me feel a little dizzy," said Grandma, "so I went outside for a breath of fresh air. It was a magical night. There was a full moon, and thousands of stars twinkled in the sky. That's when I saw him."

"Who, Grandma?" asked Hazel and Hilary.

"The Ring-tailed Rabbit!" said Grandma.

"You really saw him!" Hilary gasped. "Do you believe what everyone says—that he brings good luck wherever he goes?"

"Of course," Grandma said. "Didn't you ever hear about the rainless summer?"

"No, Grandma," the sisters said. "Please tell us!"

"Well, it was a terrible thing," Grandma said. "The crops didn't grow and there was nothing to eat. One moonlit night the Ring-tailed Rabbit hopped through the fields. The next morning the dried-up fields were filled with row after row of carrots and green vegetables."

"How did he do that?" asked Hazel.

"Nobody knows, dear," Grandma answered. "But every time he appears something wonderful happens."

"Did something wonderful happen when you saw him?" Hilary asked.

"Well, I had heard many stories about the Ring-tailed Rabbit," said Grandma, "but I had never seen him myself. So you can imagine my surprise when there he was, big as life, taking a drink from the goldfish pond at the Cottontail Ball."

"What did you do?" asked the sisters.

"Absolutely nothing," said Grandma. "My heart was racing and my mouth was dry. I couldn't even speak. The Ring-tailed Rabbit looked up at me and winked. Then he was gone. But I knew right then and there that it was my turn for a little of that Ring-tailed Rabbit's magic. Something lucky was going to happen to me very soon.

"I went back inside to the dance," continued Grandma, "and a few minutes later I met your grandfather for the very first time. He appeared at my side, introduced himself, and asked me to dance. So, you see, the Ring-tailed Rabbit really does bring good luck," added Grandma warmly.

Then Grandma kissed Hilary and Hazel good night. The sisters fell asleep and began spinning their own sweet dreams about the Ring-tailed Rabbit.